The Case Of The

Haunted Camp™

The New Adventures of MARY-KATE & ASHLEY™

The Case Of The
Haunted Camp™

by Nina Alexander

DUALSTAR PUBLICATIONS PARACHUTE PRESS

SCHOLASTIC INC.

New York   Toronto   London   Auckland   Sydney

DUALSTAR PUBLICATIONS   PARACHUTE PRESS

Dualstar Publications
c/o Thorne and Company
1801 Century Park East
Los Angeles, CA 90067

Parachute Press
156 Fifth Avenue
Suite 325
New York, NY 10010

Published by Scholastic Inc.

With special thanks to Robert Thorne and Harold Weitzberg.

Printed in the U.S.A.
June 1998
ISBN: 0-590-29397-4
A B C D E F G H I J

CAMP BIG BEAR, HERE WE COME!

"**H**ello. You have reached the office of the Olsen and Olsen Mystery Agency. Detectives Mary-Kate and Ashley Olsen can't come to the phone right now. But leave a message and we'll call you as soon as we get back from summer camp."

I pressed the button to stop the recording. Then I turned to my sister, Ashley. "How was that?" I asked.

"Good job, Mary-Kate," Ashley replied. She picked up a sheet of light blue paper from her desk. THINGS TO DO BEFORE WE LEAVE FOR CAMP was printed neatly on top in all capital letters.

Ashley put a check mark next to number 14 on the list—record new phone message. There were only two things left to do. Number 15—load car. And number 16—get in car and put on seat belts.

Ashley makes lists for everything. She's very organized. And thoughtful. And organized. And logical. And organized.

I'm not logical at all. At least that's what Ashley tells me.

Ashley and I are different in almost every way, except one—we look exactly alike. That's because we're twins! We both have strawberry-blond hair and big blue eyes. Sometimes people can't even tell us apart.

"Should I tell Dad we're ready for him to come and get our trunks?" Ashley asked. We headed downstairs to our bedroom.

"I just have to put in a few more things," I

said. I grabbed a framed photo of our basset hound, Clue, from my dresser and shoved it into my trunk. Then I tossed in a baseball, two packs of bubble gum, a necklace made out of paper clips, my favorite stuffed walrus, and a key ring with all the keys I've found in my life.

Ashley shook her head. "None of those things is on the list we got from Camp Big Bear. The list said: 'Three pairs shorts, one pair jeans, two bathing suits—'"

I stared at her. "You *memorized* the list?" I cried.

"I just want to be prepared," Ashley said. "I've never been to camp before."

"Neither have I," I reminded her. "That's why I'm bringing so much stuff. I don't know what I'll need." I tried to close my trunk. The lid wouldn't shut. The trunk was too full.

"I doubt you'll need a paper clip necklace," Ashley said.

"Maybe we'll have a fancy party and I'll need my best jewelry," I teased.

"I wonder what camp will really be like," Ashley said. "Do you think we'll have fun? Do you think the other campers will be nice? Do you think we'll miss Mom and Dad a lot? Do you think the food will be icky? Do you think—"

"You're doing it again." I moaned.

"What?" Ashley asked.

"You're making another one of your lists!" I exclaimed. I sat on the lid of my trunk. It still wouldn't close.

"Well, I guess I'm a little nervous," Ashley admitted.

"Me, too," I said. "But Camp Big Bear looked really cool in the pictures we saw." I bounced up and down on the lid of my trunk. It *still* wouldn't close.

"Yeah," Ashley agreed. "The lake looked awesome. I can't wait to go canoeing."

"I can't wait to tell ghost stories around the campfire," I said.

"I can't wait to play baseball, and take a

nature hike, and learn how to—"

"Ashley, can you stop making lists for one second and help me close my trunk?" I begged.

Ashley sat down next to me on the trunk, and the lid closed with a *click*.

"I hope you didn't forget anything," she said. "You won't be able to fit one more thing in that trunk."

"Oh, no! I did forget something—my mini tape recorder!" I exclaimed.

Great-grandma Olive gave me the tape recorder so I could take notes when Ashley and I are on a case. She likes to help us with our detective work.

"You won't need your tape recorder," Ashley said. "We're on vacation. We won't be trying to solve a mystery at camp."

"You never know," I answered. I tucked the tape recorder into my backpack. "A mystery can happen anywhere—even at camp!"

2

WE DON'T BELONG HERE

"**B**ye, Mom! Bye, Dad! Bye, Trent! Bye, Lizzie!" Ashley took a deep breath. "Bye, Clue!"

I waved with both hands until our car disappeared around the curve in Camp Big Bear's driveway.

"I miss everybody already," I said.

"Me, too," Ashley agreed. "But Camp Big Bear looks awesome!"

I unzipped the outside pocket of my suitcase and pulled out my mini tape recorder.

"This is Mary-Kate Olsen," I said into the tiny speaker. "It's two o'clock in the afternoon. We've just arrived at Camp Big Bear. It's sunny and cold here in the mountains."

I paused to rub my arms. Then I looked around and continued. "There are lots of other kids here. We're standing in front of a big log cabin."

"It's not really a cabin," Ashley corrected me. "Cabins are smaller."

I rolled my eyes. "We're standing in front of a long *building* made out of logs," I said. "It appears to be the main camp building. Olsen and Olsen to investigate this immediately." I snapped off the recorder.

"Come on," Ashley said. "Put that away. We're not even on a case."

"Hi," a voice said behind us. "This must be your first time at Camp Big Bear."

Ashley and I whirled around. A slender girl about our age was standing there. She had long, wavy brown hair and a friendly smile.

"You're right!" Ashley exclaimed. "But how could you tell?"

The girl laughed. "This is my third summer at Camp Big Bear, so I know everyone who's been here before. My name is Mia. I'm one of the official meet-and-greeters. You can ask me any questions you want to about the camp."

"I'm Ashley, and this is my sister Mary-Kate," Ashley said.

"You're lucky," I told Mia. "Our parents wouldn't let us come to sleepaway camp until this year."

"You'll love it," Mia said. "It's tons of fun. The other campers are really cool."

A tall girl with curly, dark hair rushed past us. She had a big scowl on her face.

"Hi, Jenny!" Mia called after her.

The girl spun around. "Oh, hi, Mia," she muttered.

"I didn't think you were coming back to camp this year," Mia said.

"I didn't want to come back to this stupid

camp," Jenny answered. "But my parents made me." She stomped away.

"Well, *most* of the campers are really cool," Mia whispered.

It didn't take a detective to guess that Mia didn't think Jenny was one of the cool campers.

"Jenny was one of my bunk mates last year," Mia told us. "Her parents *made* her come to camp, and she hated it. Finally she got sick, and they sent her home."

"Wow," Ashley said. "Why did she hate it so much?"

Ashley sounded a little nervous, and I knew why—if Jenny hated camp, maybe we would, too!

"Jenny complained about *everything*. I don't think there was one thing she liked," Mia answered. "But don't worry. Everyone else loves Camp Big Bear, and so will you!"

Mia pointed to the main building. "The first thing you have to do is go inside and find out your cabin number. Sandy hung a list of campers and cabins in the mess hall."

"I have two questions for you, Mia," Ashley said. "Number one: What's a mess hall?"

"And number two: Who's Sandy?" I asked.

Ashley gave me a high-five.

Mia stared back and forth between Ashley and me. "How did you do that?" she asked.

"Sometimes I know exactly what Ashley's thinking," I said.

"And sometimes *I* know exactly what Mary-Kate's thinking," Ashley added. "That's what makes us a great team!"

Mia laughed. "Number one: The mess hall is where we eat. It's in the main building there. The arts and crafts room and the rec room are there, too," she explained.

"Number two: Sandy Stevens is the head counselor," Mia continued. "She's really great. She used to work at Camp Condor, the boys' camp across the woods from us. I'm really glad she's here now."

"Let's go check it out, Ashley," I said. "Maybe we're in Mia's cabin."

"You're not," Mia said. "I already checked. All my bunk mates are people I know from last year. Too bad." She shrugged. "But maybe we'll be neighbors."

She led the way inside the main building. We entered a huge room full of long wooden tables and long wooden benches. Campers wandered around everywhere.

A short, skinny woman stood in the middle of the room, holding a clipboard. She had dark blond hair.

"That's Sandy," Mia said. "The list of cabin assignments is over on that bulletin board." She pointed to the back wall.

I ran over and studied the list. It was in alphabetical order. Ah-ha! Ashley and I were in Cabin 7.

I ran back across the room. Ashley was still talking to Mia. I tugged on her arm eagerly. "Come on," I told her. "Let's go check out our cabin. I can't wait to see it!"

We said good-bye to Mia and headed outside. I pulled out my mini tape recorder again as we walked.

"There's a smooth dirt trail leading from the main building down toward the lake," I said into the microphone. "I see lots of cool stuff around here—a playground, a volleyball net, and a big fire pit. Also, lots and lots of trees.

"Just ahead I can see a row of small, square wooden buildings with steep roofs. I suspect they are the cabins."

There were numbers painted on the doors of each cabin. The first one we came to was number one. Then came number two. Then three. You get the idea.

We hurried past Cabin 6. "Cabin Seven must be around this bend in the trail," Ashley said.

I raced around the curve in the trail. Ashley was right behind me. "You're right! Here it is!" I exclaimed. I tried the cabin door. But it wouldn't budge.

Ashley tried the door, too. She frowned. "That's strange," she said. "We're locked out of our own cabin."

"Maybe the door is stuck." I wiggled the knob and gave a hard yank. But the door still didn't open.

Ashley walked around to the side of the cabin. "Mary-Kate, there's no glass in one of the windows over here," she called. "Just a screen. We could pull it off and climb in."

I let go of the doorknob and raced over to Ashley. Within seconds, we had the screen off. It was kind of grimy. I set it carefully on the ground outside the cabin. Then I wiped my hands on my shorts.

"Give me a boost, okay?" I said.

Ashley hoisted me up, and I scrambled over the windowsill. I dropped to the floor and looked around.

"Oh, no!" I gasped.

"What?" Ashley cried. "Help me in so I can

see, too!" She struggled to push herself through the window.

I grabbed her by the wrists and pulled her inside. Ashley's eyes grew wide as she stared around the cabin. "We're supposed to live in here?" she whispered.

"No way!" I cried. "Mom and Dad wouldn't send us to a place like this! Would they?"

3

GO HOME!

Spiderwebs hung from every corner of the cabin. The floor was coated with dirt and leaves. Hardly any sunlight made its way through the filthy windows.

"Mary-Kate, look," Ashley whispered. She pointed to a bed across the room. It looked ready for someone to sleep in. A nightgown and slippers—gray with dust—lay at the foot. The covers were turned down. And a teddy bear sat on the pillow. Spiderwebs were wrapped around its face.

I slowly walked over to the bed. The wooden floorboards squeaked with each step I took.

"Maybe we should just go," Ashley said. "Maybe we should call Mom and Dad and ask them to take us home. They wouldn't have left us here if they knew what it was like."

I wanted to leave. But I couldn't. Not yet. I had to take a closer look. I had to figure out if someone was really living in this horrible cabin.

I ran my finger over the blanket, wiping a clean spot in the dust. No one has touched this for a very long time, I realized.

I picked up the teddy bear and studied it. "Who left you here?" I asked.

A fat brown spider crawled out of the teddy bear's ear and skittered up my arm. Ewww! I flicked the spider away and threw the teddy bear across the room.

"Let's get out of here—now!" I cried.

We raced to the door. I shoved it open.

Ashley and I ran into the bright, cheerful sunlight.

"Hey, you two! Stay away from there!" a girl yelled.

I spun toward her. It was Jenny, the scowling girl Ashley and I met in the main building.

"Did you see the ghost?" Jenny cried.

"What ghost?" I exclaimed.

Jenny stared at Ashley and me. "Didn't anyone warn you about the ghost of Cabin Seven?" she asked.

"Ghost! No one said anything about a ghost!" Ashley answered.

"Come on," Jenny said. "I'll tell you everything. But we have to get away from here."

We ran over to a picnic table near the playground. Ashley and I sat down across from Jenny.

"You two are in danger," Jenny said. "You better go home right now, before it's too late."

"What are you talking about?" I demanded.

Jenny took a deep breath. "Cabin Seven is

haunted," she said. "No one is allowed in there."

"But we were assigned to Cabin Seven!" I protested.

Jenny shook her head. "Someone must have made a mistake. No one stays in the ghost's cabin."

"I don't believe in ghosts," Ashley said. She didn't sound completely sure.

I *did* believe in ghosts. And Cabin 7 looked exactly like the kind of place a ghost would live!

"The ghost is going to be very angry that you two broke into her cabin," Jenny continued. "I know she's going to come after you— tonight! You won't be safe as long as you stay at Camp Big Bear."

4

THE ANGRY GHOST

"I don't think I want to stay here," I told Ashley. "Maybe Mom and Dad can come and pick us up before it gets dark."

"That's a good idea," Jenny said. "I think everyone at camp should go home. It's not safe here now that you made the ghost angry."

A plump woman with shiny black hair rushed over to us. "You must be Mary-Kate and Ashley Olsen, right?"

"That's us!" Ashley answered.

"I'm Ellie, your counselor," the woman said.

"Come on, let me show you where you'll be living this week."

Ellie led us into the cabin directly across from the playground. Jenny followed us.

"We thought we were in Cabin Seven. We went there first by mistake," Ashley told her.

Ellie shook her head. "Sandy has the worst handwriting. No wonder you got confused," she said. "Well, better late than never. Welcome to Cabin One!"

She pointed to a girl with light blond hair. "That's Brittany." Brittany grinned at us—and I could see that her teeth were covered in purple braces.

"And you already know Jenny," Ellie said. "That bunk bed over by the window is free," she continued. "And your trunks are already here. They're right over by the bed."

I didn't want a bunk. I didn't want to sleep here. I wanted to go home!

"I want to call my parents," I blurted out.

"Is something wrong?" Ellie asked.

"Ashley and I went into Cabin Seven. We didn't know we weren't supposed to. Now the ghost is angry and it's going to come after us!" I explained in a rush. "I want to go home."

Brittany started to giggle.

Ellie shook her head. "You have nothing to worry about, Mary-Kate," she told me. "Cabin Seven isn't haunted. There is no ghost. That's just a story we tell around the campfire."

Ashley nudged me. "I told you there was no ghost, Mary-Kate."

"If Cabin Seven isn't haunted, then why doesn't anyone ever go in there?" Jenny demanded.

"Do you want to know the *real* reason everyone is afraid to go into Cabin Seven?" Ellie asked.

I nodded. I had to know.

"Skunks!" Ellie announced. "A family of skunks lives under Cabin Seven. We tried everything, but we couldn't get them to move. That's why we don't use that cabin anymore!"

Ashley smiled. "I knew there was a logical explanation," she said.

I shook my head. "We went inside," I said. "We saw the ghost's nightgown and slippers and even her teddy bear."

"I'll tell you a secret," Ellie said. "The counselors put those things into Cabin Seven. All the campers love the story of the Camp Big Bear ghost. So we decided to make it seem even more real—just for fun."

"That makes sense," Ashley said.

"Good. I have to run over to the main building for a minute," Ellie told us. "Why don't you get settled, then I'll come back and fill all of you in on everything you need to know about Camp Big Bear." She hurried out of the cabin and shut the door behind her.

"See, Mary-Kate? We have nothing to worry about," Ashley said. "The worst thing skunks could do to us is make us smell really bad!"

"You don't believe that stupid story about the stupid skunks, do you?" Jenny demanded.

"The camp probably makes all the counselors tell that story—or everyone would leave!"

Brittany pushed her white-blond hair away from her face. "I'm totally confused."

"Forget everything Ellie just told you," Jenny said. "Cabin Seven *is* haunted. Whenever anyone goes into that cabin, the ghost gets *angry*."

Jenny leaned close to Brittany. "I hope the ghost leaves us alone when it comes after them." Jenny pointed to us.

I felt my heart give a hard thud in my chest.

"Only babies believe in ghosts," Brittany answered.

"Yeah," Ashley agreed.

Jenny crossed her arms over her chest and glared at everyone. "That's what you think now," she said. "Wait until the cookout tonight. Wait until you hear Sandy tell the story of the ghost in Cabin Seven."

5

CAMPFIRE STORY

"**M**ary-Kate, your marshmallow is on fire," Mia told me.

Brittany grabbed my stick and pulled my black marshmallow out of the flames.

Ashley shook her head. "You're still thinking about that ghost, aren't you?" she whispered. "You're missing all the fun of the cookout."

She was right. I was thinking about the ghost. I couldn't help it. What if what Jenny said was true? What if there really was a ghost in Cabin 7? And what if it was really mad at me and Ashley? What if—

"Attention, campers," Sandy called. "It's time for a Camp Big Bear first-night tradition." She grinned.

"Ghost stories!" Mia and all the other returning campers shouted.

Jenny poked me in the arm. "Now you're going to hear the *truth* about Cabin Seven," she whispered.

"Everybody, listen," Sandy continued. "I'm going to tell you about the ghost in Cabin Seven. But I'm warning you. It's a pretty scary story."

I scooted a little closer to Ashley. I was glad all the other campers were sitting around me. I was especially glad Ellie, our counselor, was close by.

Sandy's voice was low and spooky as she began her tale. "One summer, many years ago," she said, "a girl named Emma came to Camp Big Bear. She loved it here. She loved swimming, and hiking, and singing around the campfire. She loved the trees and the mountains and the lake. She especially loved swinging on the tire swing in the playground. It was Emma's favorite thing to do."

I grabbed Ashley's arm and held on tight.

"Come on, Mary-Kate. It's just a story," Ashley whispered.

"That's not what Jenny said!" I whispered back.

"One night," Sandy continued, "Emma left her bunk in Cabin Seven late. Her bunk mates tried to stop her. 'It's too late to go outside,' they warned her. 'Strange creatures live in the mountains around the camp—creatures who are half wolf and half bear. They might come after you. Don't go out!' they told Emma."

I shivered as I imagined an animal with long, razor-sharp claws and huge teeth dripping with saliva. I pictured it as big as a bear but as fast as a wolf.

"'I'm not afraid,' Emma replied. 'I'll be fine.'

She ran out the door of her cabin. When her bunk mates heard the tire swing begin to creak, they felt better. As long as they could hear the swing creaking, they knew Emma was okay. *Creeeak. Creeeak. Creeeak.*

"Emma's bunk mates turned out the lights in their cabin and went back to bed. *Creeeak. Creeeak. Creeeak.*

"Then Emma's bunk mates heard something that sent chills through them. 'Helllp meeeee!' Emma screamed—a long, shrill scream of pure terror. Her bunk mates leaped out of bed and raced to the playground."

Sandy paused. "It was too late. The swing was empty. Emma was gone. And she was never seen again."

I gasped.

"To this day, some people claim that they hear the sound of the tire swing creaking late, late at night. When they look outside—no one is there!"

My gooey marshmallow slipped out of my

fingers and fell into the dirt.

"Now, some of you might be curious about Cabin Seven. You might want to go inside and see for yourself where Emma lived," Sandy said. "But going into Cabin Seven would be a bad idea—a very bad idea."

Sandy leaned closer to the fire. The flames threw spooky shadows on her face.

"You see, Emma likes to be alone, and she gets very angry when anyone enters her cabin," Sandy said.

"A few years ago one of our campers who didn't believe in ghosts broke into Cabin Seven."

Sandy shook her head. "That was a bad summer. Emma was very upset. All our canoes were set adrift in the lake. The volleyball net was torn down and ripped to shreds. Campers found bugs and leaves and dirt stuffed into their sleeping bags."

"See, I told you," Jenny whispered into my ear.

"It's late," Sandy said. "This isn't a story I should be telling you right before you go to sleep. Let's turn in."

"Finish the story!" Mia cried.

"Yes," the other campers called. "Finish the story. Tell us what happened to the girl who broke into cabin seven."

"No one really knows what happened to her," Sandy admitted. "One morning, the camper was gone. On her pillow was a pink hair ribbon—the same kind of pink hair ribbon that Emma always used to wear."

I wrapped my arms around myself. I felt cold all over.

"We searched everywhere," Sandy told us. "But we never found her."

"That's going to happen to you and your sister," Jenny whispered to me. "One night Emma is going to come for you—and you'll never be seen again."

6

CREAK, CREAK, CREAK

I lay in the bottom bunk that night and stared out the window. The moonlight was so bright, I could see everything in the playground—including the tire swing.

"Ashley, do you think Emma will come tonight?" I whispered.

Ashley didn't answer.

I gave the top bunk a gentle kick. "Ashley, I said, do you think the ghost is going to come tonight? We broke into her cabin—just like the girl in the story!"

"Of course Emma is going to come," I heard someone whisper from across the room. "It's not safe for any of us to stay in this cabin."

I sighed. I didn't want to talk to Jenny. I wanted to talk to Ashley. But Ashley was sound asleep.

I put my head under the covers and flicked on my flashlight. I took it to bed with me—just in case.

I shone the light on my watch. It was almost ten. What time did ghosts get up? Midnight?

Think of something else, I ordered myself. I tried to imagine what everyone in my family was doing right now.

I knew what Ashley was doing—sleeping. Our little sister, Lizzie, was definitely sleeping too.

Our big brother, Trent, *should* be sleeping. His bedtime was nine o'clock. But knowing Trent, he was still awake, probably playing his mini video game under the covers.

Mom and Dad were probably watching the news or something. I'll just pretend they are in the next room right now, I thought.

I clicked off the flashlight and stuck it under my pillow. Then I closed my eyes.

The cabin was completely silent now. I think even Jenny was asleep. There wasn't one sound coming from her bed.

Creeeak. Creeeak. Creeeak.

I sat up fast. I grabbed my mini tape recorder. It was tucked under my pillow right next to my flashlight—just in case.

"Th-there's a creaking sound coming from outside the cabin," I whispered into the recorder. It sounds like—like the tire swing."

Creeeak. Creeeak. Creeeak.

I pulled in a long, deep breath. "Maybe it's Emma's tire swing."

I knew I should look out the window. That's what any good detective would do. But I really, really did not want to see a ghost!

On the count of three, I'll look.

One.

Creeeak.

Two.

Creeeak.

Three.

Creeeak.

I jerked my head toward the window. My hand trembled as I brought the tape recorder back up to my lips.

"I see the tire swing. It's moving. But nobody is in it!"

It's the ghost! I thought.

Wait. Ashley doesn't believe in ghosts, I reminded myself. Maybe she's right. Maybe ghosts aren't real.

Creeeak. Creeeak. Creeeak.

I stared out at the rocking swing.

This is a case for Olsen and Olsen, I decided. And it is our most important case yet—because our lives might depend on solving it!

Do You Believe
in Ghosts?

I sprang out of bed. I stood on tiptoe and shook Ashley's shoulder.

"What?" she mumbled.

"The tire swing! It's moving back and forth all by itself!" I cried. "The ghost is out there—right now!"

Ashley gave a little squeak and sat straight up in bed. She pushed her face against the window.

"Look, Mary-Kate. The swing isn't moving." Ashley scooted back so I could see outside.

"Maybe you dreamed it," she suggested. "That ghost story probably gave you a nightmare."

"I wasn't asleep," I told her. "I'm positive I was awake. Totally positive."

"Okay, let's try to think like detectives," Ashley said. "What else could have made the swing move?"

She thought for a moment. "I know! The wind!" she exclaimed.

I checked the window. "The trees aren't moving," I answered. "That means there isn't any wind."

"Hmmm. Maybe an animal walked by and bumped into the swing. Like a deer or something," Ashley said. "Go to sleep, Mary Kate," she told me. There is *no* ghost."

Ashley wouldn't believe there was a ghost at Camp Big Bear unless we had *all* the facts. And we didn't have any.

At least not yet.

* * *

"Hurry up, Mary-Kate. I can't wait to learn to canoe," Ashley said. She gave a little skip as we headed to the lake.

I trudged down the trail after her.

"What's wrong, Mary-Kate?" Mia asked. She gave a big yawn. "Don't you want to go canoeing?"

"Canoeing is stupid," Jenny muttered before I could answer.

"No, it's not. It's really fun," Brittany said. "I went last summer, and it was awesome!"

"I'm worried about the ghost," I told Mia. "Ashley and I went into Cabin Seven yesterday. It was a mistake. We thought it was *our* cabin. We didn't mean to make Emma angry."

"You went into Cabin Seven? I can't believe you went into Cabin Seven!" Mia cried.

"You don't really believe in the ghost, do you?" Brittany demanded.

"I…I guess not," Mia said. But she sounded really worried.

"I don't either," Ashley said.

"I do!" Jenny declared. "People who don't believe in ghosts are stupid."

"Maybe Ashley and I could apologize to Emma," I said. "We could tell her we didn't know she didn't like anyone to go in her cabin."

"That's a great idea!" Mia exclaimed.

I started to feel a teeny, tiny bit better.

"There's no such thing as ghosts—so I can't apologize to one," Ashley said firmly.

I felt a whole lot worse. If Ashley wouldn't apologize, my plan wouldn't work. We both went into Cabin 7—so we would both have to apologize to Emma.

We hiked around a bend in the trail, and the lake came into view.

"Oh, no!" Mia exclaimed. "Look at that!" She pointed toward the lake.

I stared at the sparkling blue-green water. "What?" I asked.

"The canoes! Someone untied the canoes!" Mia cried.

She was right! Canoes bobbed up and down in the middle of the lake.

Red ones. Blue ones. Green ones. Yellow ones. And all of them were empty.

"Emma untied them," Jenny whispered. "It's exactly what she did last time someone broke into her cabin!"

I felt my knees begin to tremble. I couldn't stop staring at the canoes. "Ashley, do you still say there's no such thing as ghosts?"

8

HELP ME!

"**M**ary-Kate, I know you're really scared," Ashley said. "But we have to be logical. A ghost isn't the only explanation for how the canoes got out in the middle of the lake."

"Yeah," Brittany agreed. "Maybe whoever tied up the canoes didn't do a good job, and the knots came loose."

"That's stupid," Jenny said. "The same person didn't tie up every one of those canoes. Do you think everyone at Camp Big Bear ties bad knots? That's really stupid!"

"And even if the knots *were* all bad, they wouldn't all come loose at exactly the same time. It isn't *logical*," I told Ashley.

"You're right, Mary-Kate," Ashley said. "It isn't logical!"

Yes! I thought. She believes me now!

"Someone must have untied the canoes," Ashley continued. "But that *doesn't* mean the ghost untied them."

"Maybe you're right, Ashley," I said. "Maybe the ghost didn't untie the canoes. But, then— who did? And why?"

Ashley frowned, the way she does when she's thinking hard.

"I don't know," she admitted.

"This is a case for Olsen and Olsen!" I exclaimed. "Lucky for us I brought my tape recorder."

"I think you're right," Ashley agreed. "I wonder if Ellie would lend me a notebook so I can take notes." She hurried over to our counselor to ask her.

Yes, yes, yes! Ashley was on the case!

I was positive Olsen and Olsen could prove that the ghost was real. And once Ashley knew the ghost was real, she would apologize.

Case closed! Problem solved!

Unless...unless the ghost came and took me and Ashley away before we finished our investigation!

"We've been so busy today, I've hardly had a second to think about the case." Ashley flipped open her notebook.

"I know," I answered. "It's hard to be a good detective when you're having so much fun."

I *did* have fun. I decided not to let the ghost ruin my very first full day at camp.

There was something to do every second— and I loved it all. Ashley and I went swimming, played a baseball game, and made a braided collar for our basset hound, Clue.

Plus all the kids in our bunk helped make dinner. Even that was fun, except that Jenny kept complaining. She said the aprons we wore were stupid. She said cooking was stupid. She even said spaghetti was stupid!

"So, what do we have so far?" I asked Ashley.

Ashley flipped open her notebook and read over her lists. "Not much," she admitted. "I can't believe we didn't find one clue by the docks where the canoes were tied."

As soon as I convinced Ashley to take the case, she searched every inch of the dock. She looked for anything that seemed out of place—a scrap of cloth, a piece of paper, an unusual footprint, *anything*.

I helped Ashley, but I knew we wouldn't find anything. Ghosts don't leave clues.

Then Ashley studied the canoe ropes. She wanted to try and take fingerprints off them, but the ropes were too wet.

I wanted to tell Ashley that there wouldn't be any fingerprints—because ghosts don't have fingers! But Ashley didn't believe in ghosts.

At least not yet!

Ashley sighed and closed the notebook. "We'll have to search for more clues tomorrow," she said.

"Can I see?" Brittany asked. She reached out for the notebook.

Ashley glanced at me. I nodded.

Usually Ashley and I don't talk about our cases with other people. But Brittany was our bunk mate.

"Wow, you write down *everything*. You wrote down exactly how many canoes were set loose," Brittany said. "You even wrote down the colors of the canoes!"

"I just wish there was more to write down." Ashley sighed again. "We'll never be able to crack this case if we don't find more clues!"

"You'll get a lot more clues tonight," Jenny called from across the room. She put her toothbrush and toothpaste in her suitcase and slammed the lid shut.

Everyone else had totally unpacked all their stuff. But Jenny's suitcase was still full.

"What do you mean?" Ashley asked.

"I mean the ghost is going to come back tonight and do something bad," Jenny answered. "Then you'll have lots of clues to write down in your stupid notebook."

"I have a clue for you, Jenny," Brittany said. She picked up her pillow and threw it at Jenny's head.

"Pillow fight!" I yelled.

I grabbed my pillow and threw it at Brittany. Brittany picked it up and threw it at Ashley.

"Pillow fights are stupid," Jenny muttered.

We all threw our pillows at Jenny.

"*Helllp me!*" a voice wailed.

I felt the hair on the back of my neck stand on end.

"*Helllp me!*" the voice cried again.

"W-what was that?" Brittany stammered.

"Are you crazy? It was the ghost!" Jenny

answered. She glared at us.

I couldn't say anything. My mouth felt too dry to talk.

"*Helllp me!*"

The wail sounded louder. And even closer.

"It's the ghost!" Jenny shrieked. "It's coming to get us! And it's all your fault!" She glared at Ashley and me. "You made it angry. Now it's after us all!"

Ashley grabbed me by the arm. "Where's your tape recorder?" Ashley cried. "Quick! Turn it on—this is definitely a clue!"

That's Ashley. Even in the middle of a ghost attack, she remembers to act like a detective.

I grabbed the recorder from under my pillow and switched it on.

"*Helllp meeee!*"

"Go away!" Brittany screamed. "Leave us alone!"

"*Helllp meeee!*"

The voice sounded softer this time.

Farther away.

Silence filled the cabin.

"Do you think it's gone?" Ashley finally whispered.

I held my breath and listened hard. All I heard was a few crickets chirping.

"It's gone," Jenny said, her voice quavering. "But not for long. It will be back—I know it!"

9

MARY-KATE
MAKES A MOVIE

"**W**ait until you hear this secret," Mia whispered. She sat down across the table from Ashley and me.

"What?" I mumbled. I swallowed a bite of my cheese omelette.

"My bunk made breakfast this morning, and I forgot my hat in the kitchen," Mia said.

"That's a stupid secret!" Jenny snapped.

Mia rolled her eyes. "That's not the secret, Jenny. The secret is what I heard Sandy tell one of other counselors when I went to get my hat," Mia explained.

"Tell us," Brittany said. She shoved her light blond hair behind her ears and stared at Mia. "We have to hear the secret!"

"Sandy said that we couldn't play volleyball today—because the volleyball net was ripped to shreds last night!" Mia exclaimed.

I dropped my fork onto the floor. "It's just like the story," I whispered. I turned to Ashley. "Now *you* have to believe there is a ghost at camp!"

"I guess it's possible that there might be a real ghost," Ashley admitted. She pushed her plate away. She hadn't eaten much.

Jenny glared at Ashley from across the table. "There *might* be a ghost?" she repeated. "What more evidence do you need? The canoes were set loose and the volleyball net was ripped up. That's exactly what Emma did last time!"

Brittany nodded. "I didn't believe there was a ghost at first. But we all heard it outside our cabin last night. Mary-Kate even got the ghost on tape."

"You got the ghost on tape?" Mia cried. "Can I hear it?"

.   I pulled my mini tape recorder out of my jacket pocket and clicked it on. "*Helllp meee!*" the voice wailed.

I got scared all over again just listening to the tape.

Mia shivered. "That has to be the ghost," she told Ashley. "It has to be."

"I'm still not positive," Ashley said. "We need more evidence."

"But what kind of evidence?" I asked.

"Attention, everybody," Sandy called from the front of the mess hall. "I just have a couple announcements. First, we're going to compete against the Camp Condor boys in a mini Olympics on Friday. There are sign-up sheets on the bulletin board for the events," she said.

"And tonight is movie night," Sandy went on. "We have a collection of videos in the rec room. We'll take a vote at dinner on which movie to show. Have a great day, everyone!"

"I hope no one wants to see a scary movie," Brittany mumbled. "I'm not ready for another scary night."

"I think a scary movie is a great idea!" I exclaimed.

Ashley stared at me. "You do?" she asked.

I nodded. "Yeah, a scary movie is the perfect way to get more evidence!" I leaned close, and told them my plan.

I peered through the viewfinder of the video camera. I could see the swing perfectly. "The moon gives plenty of light for our movie," I announced.

"You're brilliant, Mary-Kate," Ashley said. "Now all we have to do is push the record button and go to sleep. In the morning we'll have the ghost on film!"

We told Ellie and Sandy that we wanted to make a movie of the owls that lived at Camp

Big Bear.

We didn't think they would like the idea of us trying to make our own scary ghost movie!

While we were talking to Sandy, Ashley asked her if the counselors ever pretended to be the ghost—just for fun!

Sandy laughed—and said no way!

"I don't know if this plan to videotape the ghost will work," Brittany said. "Isn't the ghost invisible?"

"We'll still be able to see if the swing moves," Ashley told her. "And we'll be able to tell if the wind is strong enough to move the swing by studying the trees in the background."

"And if an animal moves the swing, we'll see that, too," I added. "This movie will give us a lot of new evidence."

Ellie swung open the door and stepped into the cabin. "Everybody ready for lights out?" she asked.

I pushed the record button on the video

camera and climbed into my bottom bunk. "Ready," I answered.

"I hope you get some owls on your tape," Ellie said. Then she flipped off the lights.

Creeeak. Creeeak.

I rolled over and pulled my pillow over my head. I wished that creaking would stop. I was trying to sleep.

Creeeak. Creeeak.

Wait! That's the tire swing!

I bolted up in bed.

I stared out the window, but the creaking had stopped. The tire hung motionless.

I scrambled out of bed and checked the video camera. The little red light was on, and that meant the camera was still recording. Yes!

"Ashley, get up! The ghost was out there," I whispered.

"Wha-huh?" Ashley rubbed her eyes. "What time is it?"

I checked my watch. "It's almost six. It will

be light any minute. Let's go watch the tape now—before it's time for everyone to get up."

I couldn't wait to prove to Ashley once and for all that there really was a ghost. Then we could apologize to Emma—and everything would be okay again.

I tiptoed over to Brittany's bed and shook her shoulder. "Get dressed," I whispered. "It's time to watch the tape."

Brittany jumped up so fast, she hit her head on the top bunk of her bed. "Ouch!" she cried.

"Shhh. We don't want to wake up Ellie," I said.

"You already woke *me* up," Jenny complained. "I'm coming with you."

"Fine," Ashley said. "Just be quiet."

I pulled on my sneakers and my jacket, then I slid the videotape out of the camera. When everyone was dressed, I grabbed my flashlight and we tiptoed out of the cabin.

I flipped my flashlight on. It was still really dark out.

I led the way to the main building. Usually there are a million things going on at camp in the morning. There are always kids yelling and cheering and laughing.

But it was still early. The only sounds came from our feet tromping along the path.

"It's kind of spooky out here," Brittany whispered.

"I wonder if the ghost is still around," Jenny said.

I hadn't thought of that!

I stared into the trees lining the path. I didn't see a ghost. But it was so dark, I could have missed it.

What if the ghost is out here? What if it's watching me right now?

I started to walk faster. I wanted to get inside the main building. I would feel safer there.

Jenny started to jog. So I started to jog.

Then Brittany started to run.

We all raced for the main building as fast as

we could. We dashed inside and Ashley closed the door behind us.

We rushed down the hall and into the rec room. I flipped on the lights, and right away I started to feel better. It's a lot harder to feel scared when all the lights are on.

I hurried over to the television set and popped our tape into the VCR.

"I can't believe you got the ghost on tape," Brittany said.

"I think it was a stupid thing to do," Jenny told me. "The ghost will be extra mad at you now. Ghosts don't like to be videotaped."

"Should we rewind to the beginning, or just go back a little ways?" I asked.

"Just a little ways," Ashley said. "Let's try to find the spot with the creaking you heard."

I nodded and punched the rewind button. The tape started to spin backward in the machine. I waited for a few seconds, then hit STOP. "Okay, let's try it here," I said. "Get ready to see the ghost, everyone."

I pushed PLAY. I stared at the TV screen. Finally I would have proof that there was a ghost at Camp Big Bear.

Creeeak. Creeeak. Creeeak.

The swing rocked slowly from side to side.

"See, there is no wind," I said. "It's the ghost on the swing. It's Emma."

Click!

The TV screen went black—and we all shrieked as the room plunged into darkness!

ON THE TRAIL
OF A GHOST

Jenny screamed.

"Oh, no! It's Emma. She doesn't want us to watch the tape!" Brittany cried.

"Shhhh!" Ashley held her finger to her lips. "I think I heard something."

I held my breath and listened hard.

That's when I heard something that sent a chill through me.

"*Bewaaare. Bewaaare,*" a voice howled.

"You were right, Mary-Kate," Ashley said. "There *is* a ghost. And we have to apologize to her—right now!" Ashley raced out the rec room door.

I took off after her. Brittany and Jenny were right behind me.

We ran down the hall and flew out the lodge's big front doors.

"Which way now?" Brittany gasped.

"That way!" Ashley said.

How did Ashley know which way to go? I wondered, staring into the woods. I didn't see a thing.

I followed Ashley. Suddenly I thought I saw something moving through the pine trees. I ran as fast as I could. Twigs and branches crackled beneath my feet.

I shoved my way through a big clump of bushes, then darted around two big trees. I broke out into a clearing—and saw our ghost.

"We caught you!" Ashley shouted.

11

CASE CLOSED?

"Stop right there!" Ashley cried.

Three boys in white Camp Condor T-shirts turned around and faced us. The shortest one couldn't stop giggling.

"Aren't you afraid of us?" the tallest boy cried. "We're ghosts!"

"Helllp me!" the boy with the Camp Condor baseball cap wailed.

"Bewaaaare! Bewaaaare!" the shortest boy howled. Then he broke into giggles again.

My mouth dropped open. I couldn't believe

this. "*You* are the ghost?" I demanded. "You set loose the canoes? You ripped up the volleyball net?"

"That's right," the tallest boy said.

"Well, we didn't really rip up the volleyball net," the boy in the baseball cap added. "We took your volleyball net and replaced it with this ripped-up one we had at our camp. We were going to give yours back…someday."

Ashley shook her head. "But how did you know what to do? How did you know about Emma?"

"We snuck over to your camp the night of your cookout. We heard the whole story," the boy in the baseball cap told us.

"Yeah, we were going to try and put bugs and leaves in your beds this time. That's what happened next in the story," the short boy added. "Then we saw the light in the main building, and we decided to check it out."

The tall boy smirked at us. "We heard you talking about ghosts—so we decided to turn off the power. The fuse box was right under the window."

The short boy giggled again. "You should have heard yourselves screaming!"

"*Whoooooh*. I'm a big, scary ghost," the tallest boy wailed. He danced around the clearing, waving his arms over his head.

"Oh, no! The ghost is coming after us!" the short boy squealed in a high voice. Then he cracked up.

"Come on. We have to get back to camp," the tall boy called. The three boys took off across the clearing and disappeared into the woods on the other side.

"Well, Detective Olsen, it looks like we've solved another case," Ashley said.

"You're right, Detective Olsen." I shook her hand. "Congratulations on solving the case of the haunted camp!"

"Hey, Ashley, how did you know which way to go when we started into the woods?" Brittany asked.

"Footprints!" Ashley said. "I followed a trail of footprints."

She pointed to the ground. Three sets of sneaker prints crossed the clearing. They all had different patterns. One set had a lot of little circles. One set had wavy lines. And one set had wavy lines *and* circles.

"As soon as I saw those prints, I knew we weren't dealing with a ghost," Ashley said. "Ghosts don't wear sneakers! You don't have to be a detective to know that!"

"I am going to sleep *so* much better tonight," Brittany said.

"I still think there is a real ghost," Jenny mumbled.

"The case is closed," Ashley said firmly. "We caught those boys in the act—and they confessed to everything!"

We wandered back to our cabin after the big talent show the older kids put on for us. It had been a totally terrific day.

First, we proved that there was no ghost! Then we had walnut pancakes for breakfast— my favorite. Then we went on a nature hike— and we saw a baby deer. It was the cutest thing!

After lunch we swam in the lake. Then Ashley and I made a special beaded necklace for our little sister, Lizzie.

Then we had sloppy Janes for dinner. Sandy said we shouldn't call them sloppy Joes—since we were an all-girl camp.

It really was an amazing day. I knew I was going to have good dreams tonight.

Brittany pulled open the door to our cabin—and gasped.

"M-maybe Jenny is right," she stammered. "Maybe there is a real ghost at camp. Look!"

I pushed my way past Brittany and rushed into the cabin. Leaves and twigs and dirt were scattered everywhere.

"There are snails in my sneakers!" Brittany yelled. "That's so gross!"

"My pillow is filled with rocks!" I cried.

A muddy tree branch stuck out from under the covers on my bed.

"Eww! There's a worm on my nightgown," Ashley complained.

"Is your stuff okay, Jenny?" I asked.

Jenny peeked under her blankets. She poked her pillow. She shook out her nightgown. "Everything looks okay," she mumbled. "I hope the ghost doesn't have something even worse planned for me."

"There is no ghost, Jenny," Ashley said firmly. "A ghost didn't do this." She sounded really angry. "But I know who did—those boys from Camp Condor!"

Was Ashley right? I wondered. It was logical that the Camp Condor boys played this trick on us.

But I had a hunch that there was still a *real* ghost at Camp Big Bear.

And my hunches are usually right!

A Bear Saves The Day

"You're right!" Brittany cried. "This has to be another one of the boys' pranks. They are probably laughing their heads off back at their own camp."

"There's only one thing we can do," Ashley said.

"What?" I asked.

She grinned. "We have to get revenge!"

"Okay, we're almost there," Brittany said. "I can see the lights."

"We should be quiet now, or they might hear us," I said.

We tiptoed to the edge of the woods and peered out at Camp Condor.

"It looks almost like Camp Big Bear," Ashley whispered. "Look, they have a main building made of logs just like ours. And a volleyball court. And a flagpole. And a row of cabins. And—"

"Don't start making one of your lists now," I told her.

"What are we going to do?" Jenny asked.

"Okay, now we have to split up and check the cabins," Ashley said. "We'll find the boys we're looking for faster that way."

"Good idea," Jenny said. "I'll take that cabin."

"I'll take the next one." I tiptoed over to the second cabin in the row and took a quick peek in the back window. Five boys were sitting on the floor, playing cards.

I took another look. No, they weren't our

"ghosts."

I glanced down the row of cabins and saw Brittany waving her arms back and forth. She must have found them!

I waved to Jenny. She crept over to me and we scurried over to Brittany. Ashley was already there.

"All three of the boys are in that cabin," Brittany whispered. "What do we do now?"

"I've got an idea! Let's steal their underwear!" I suggested.

"Ick!" Ashley cried. "Boys' underwear! Gross!"

We all shushed her.

"It will be great," I said. "We can throw it all in the lake or something. But first we have to get the boys out of that cabin."

Brittany's eyes widened. "How can we do that?"

I shrugged. I wasn't sure about that part. I glanced at Ashley. She shrugged, too.

"I've got it!" Jenny whispered. "I can make

great bear noises. If I growl and snarl, I bet the boys will come out."

"And we can sneak in," Ashley said. "Brilliant!"

"That's a really good idea, Jenny," I said.

Jenny grinned. It was the first time I'd seen her smile.

"I'll help you make the noises so they will be really loud," Ashley told Jenny.

"Mary-Kate and I will be on the underwear team," Brittany said.

"Give us a few minutes to sneak up next to the door, then start growling," I told Ashley and Jenny. They gave me the thumbs-up.

Brittany led the way to the front of the boys' cabin. A few seconds later we heard a loud, mean-sounding growl. Then we heard a softer, not-quite-so-mean snarl.

"Ashley needs a little practice," Brittany said.

"Yeah, but Jenny is awesome," I answered. "She's almost scaring me!"

Grrrrrrrrrr.

"What was that?" a boy cried from inside the cabin.

I gave Brittany a high-five.

Grrrrrowwwr.

"Bears!" another boy exclaimed.

"Let's check it out!" a third boy yelled.

Brittany and I pressed ourselves against the side of the cabin.

Bang! The cabin door flew open—and the boys ran right past us. They raced into the woods.

"Let's move!" I said.

I darted through the door and looked around. Three old wooden dressers lined one wall.

I raced toward the closest dresser and yanked open the top drawer. "Look at this!" I cried. I pulled out a pair of pink-and-white polka-dot boxer shorts.

"Perfect!" Brittany cried. "Those just gave me a great idea. We don't even need to bother

with anything else."

"Why not?" I asked.

"Don't you think those would look perfect on the Camp Condor flagpole?" Brittany said.

"Yes!" I exclaimed. "Let's do it!"

We raced out of the cabin. A few seconds later, Ashley and Jenny burst out of the woods and hurried over to us.

"We led the boys deeper into the woods, then we circled back here," Jenny said. She was panting hard.

"Great," I said. "Come on—we're going to hang these from the flagpole." I waved the polka-dot boxers over my head.

We raced over to the flagpole. We tried to be quiet, but we couldn't stop giggling.

I stared at the ropes and pulleys that were used to raise and lower the flags. How did they work?

I heard footsteps in the distance.

"We've got to hurry," Ashley said. "The boys are coming!"

"I can do it," Jenny said. She stepped forward and tugged on one of the ropes.

Within a few seconds, she had the boxers flying in the air.

Jenny tied the rope in place—just as the boys raced around the corner of the main building.

"Get them!" they yelled.

13

CASE OPEN

"**R**un!" Brittany shrieked. We dashed into the woods.

"Hey!" a boy cried. "Those are my shorts!"

I was laughing so hard, I could hardly run.

"We're going to get you!" another boy yelled. I heard the boys tromping through the bushes after us.

"Come on!" Ashley exclaimed with a breathless giggle. "We've got to run faster."

"Boys!" a deep voice shouted. "What's going on out here? Get back here now!"

"Their counselor caught them! They're busted!" Brittany exclaimed.

"Yesss!" I cried. I slowed down. "We did it!"

We all slapped high-fives. "We really showed those boys," Ashley bragged as we hurried back toward our own camp. "That will teach them to try and scare us!"

"Yeah," I agreed. "They'd better watch out. Next time we'll put leaves and bugs in their stuff—just like they did to us!"

"Umm…" Jenny cleared her throat. "I should probably tell you guys something."

"What?" I asked.

Jenny looked at her feet. "Well…" she said slowly. "It wasn't the boys who put those leaves and stuff in our cabin. It was me."

"Huh?" Ashley said.

We all stopped and stared at Jenny.

"What do you mean?" I demanded.

"You messed up our stuff?" Brittany glared at Jenny.

"Why?" I asked.

"I'm sorry," Jenny whispered. "It's just that I really didn't want to come to camp again this year. I hated it last year. I didn't have any fun at all."

I was confused. "What does that have to do with putting leaves and bugs in our stuff?"

"I was trying to make you think the ghost was real," Jenny explained. "I thought if everyone believed there was a ghost at camp, they'd all want to go home. Then I could go home, too."

I wasn't sure what to say. Neither was anybody else. We were all quiet for a moment.

Finally we started walking toward camp again. "Why are you telling us the truth now?" Ashley asked at last.

"Because I just decided I don't want to go home anymore," she said. "Camp is starting to be fun." She laughed. "I wish I had a picture of that boy's underwear flying in the wind!"

I looked at Ashley. She looked back at me. We both grinned. Maybe Jenny wasn't so bad after all!

"Okay, we'll forgive you," I told Jenny. I was still grinning. "But only because you do such a good bear growl!"

Jenny opened her mouth—and let out a long, loud growl.

"Camp Big Bear girls rule!" Brittany yelled.

"Camp Big Bear girls rule!" we all repeated. Jenny shouted loudest of all.

We hiked out of the woods and turned onto the dirt trail leading to the cabins.

Creeeak. Creeeak. Creeeak.

I gasped. "That sounds like—" I began.

"The tire swing," Ashley finished.

We raced around the bend in the trail, and the playground came into sight.

"Look!" I gasped. I pointed to the tire swing. There was someone on it. A pale figure dressed in a long white gown.

Jenny screamed. "Oh, no!" she cried. "It's the ghost!"

14

THE FIFTH GHOST

I gulped. I wanted to turn and run and never stop running. But I knew what I had to do.

"It's Emma," I whispered. "We have to apologize to her, Ashley. We have to explain that we didn't know Cabin Seven was her cabin."

Ashley nodded. She grabbed my hand. I could feel her fingers shaking.

We slowly started down the trail toward the playground. Jenny and Brittany followed us.

Creeeak. Creeeak. Creeeak.

Emma swung back and forth.

Did she see us coming? What was she going to do to us? Would she swoop down and take us away before we had a chance to say a word?

As we moved closer and closer, I forced myself to study Emma. She wore a long white gown that covered her from her neck to her feet.

Her feet. Did ghosts have feet? I thought they just sort of floated around—footless.

But this ghost definitely had feet and hands. She also had wavy brown hair, like Mia's.

I forced myself to take another step. "Doesn't the ghost look a lot like Mia?" I whispered to Ashley.

Ashley gasped. "The ghost looks exactly like Mia—because it *is* Mia!" she exclaimed.

I stared at the ghost. "You're right!" I answered.

"Mia, what are you doing out here?" Brittany called.

Mia didn't answer.

"I think she's asleep," Jenny said.

"She must be sleepwalking," Ashley added.

"Sleepswinging," I murmured.

"Wow. I bet if we rewound our video a little farther, we would have seen Mia on the swing," Ashley said.

Jenny took a step closer to the playground. "Should we wake her up?"

"Let's go get Sandy," Ashley suggested. "She'll know what to do."

"This is Mary-Kate Olsen," I said into my mini tape recorder. "I'm here at Camp Big Bear. And I'm happy to report that Olsen and Olsen closed another case—really closed it this time."

"Give me that." Ashley plucked the recorder out of my hand. "This is Ashley Olsen. It is three minutes after twelve in the afternoon. The weather is warm and slightly cloudy. Right now we're sitting in the mess hall. Our lunch is turkey sandwiches, potato chips, pickles. . ."

Brittany, Mia, and Jenny started to giggle. I snatched back the tape recorder. "Stop it!" I said. "We don't need any more lists. We solved the case already."

I brought the recorder to my mouth. "We found the ghost of Camp Big Bear," I said. "Actually, we found *five* ghosts. First, there were the three Camp Condor boys. They untied the canoes, and left the ripped-up volleyball net at our camp. They also made scary noises outside our cabin. And they turned off the power when we were about to watch the video tape.

"Ghost number four was Jenny," I said into my recorder. I glanced over at her and she grinned at me. "Jenny was trying to scare everyone into going home. But now she's decided she likes camp and wants to stay here with the rest of us. We're very happy about that, because no one can growl like a bear as well as Jenny."

"That's right," she said. She gave a little growl to prove it. "I don't know what I was thinking before. Camp is great! And I have a great idea for another prank we can play on those boys tonight. . . ."

"Cool!" Brittany cried.

"You can't leave me behind this time!" Mia said.

I switched off my recorder. "Do you guys mind?" I joked. "I'm trying to close out our case here."

"Sorry." Jenny grabbed a pickle and stuck the whole thing in her mouth. "I can't talk now. My mouth's too full," she mumbled.

Brittany gave a snort of laughter.

I turned the tiny machine on again. "Ghost number five was Mia," I said. "She was sleep-walking. But she won't be haunting us any-more. Sandy tied a bell on her cabin door so her bunk mates will wake up if she leaves dur-ing the night."

Mia looked embarrassed. "I can't believe I was doing that," she said. "No wonder I was so tired during the day. I spent all night on the swing!"

"One more thing," I said into the mini tape recorder. "There's still a possibility that the Cabin Seven ghost is real."

"Mary-Kate." Ashley groaned.

"We didn't find any proof that it *did* exist," I continued. "But we didn't find any proof that it *didn't* exist, either. That means the real ghost is a possible ghost number six."

Ashley shook her head at me. "I don't believe you, Mary-Kate."

"What?" I asked. "There could be a real ghost out there. Good detectives have to keep an open mind," I reminded her.

"That's not what I meant Mary-Kate," Ashley said. "I don't believe *you* finally made a nice, organized, logical list!"

Hi from both of us,

It's no secret that the Trenchcoat Twins love to solve mysteries. And we have even more brand-new mysteries for you to read! Mysteries that no one has ever seen or heard before—mysteries that even surprise us!

Ashley and I couldn't believe it when we got a call all the way from Montana. A boy named Jason White Eagle said he needed our help because someone kept robbing the ranch where he lived. First a beaded necklace was stolen, then a feathered Indian headdress, and then a big drum.

We figured out that each object was stolen on the night of a full moon. And that meant the Trenchcoat Twins had to work fast—because the next full moon was only one night away. And we were sure Jason's ranch was about to get robbed again!

Want to see how it all began? Take a look at the next page—and get a special sneak peek at The New Adventures of Mary-Kate & Ashley: The Case of the Wild Wolf River.

See you next time!

Love,

Ashley Olsen & Mary-Kate Olsen

A sneak peek at our next mystery...

The Case Of The
Wild Wolf River

"First the beaded necklace was stolen," Jason told me and Ashley as we rode our horses to the ranch house. "Then a month later, the thief came back and took the feathered headdress. And last month, the thief came back *again* and stole a big drum."

"Now only the carved wolf is left," I said.

Jason nodded. "My grandfather is so worried," he said. "The necklace, the headdress, the drum, and the wolf have been in my family for hundreds of years. They were given to my grandfather by *his* grandfather. And my grandfather promised he would give them to me some day."

"Don't worry, Jason," Ashley told him. "Mary-Kate and I will catch the thief. And we'll get back everything that was stolen."

We rode our horses past a row of small red houses made of wood.

"This is where the ranch hands and their families live," Jason explained.

"Do you think any of them could be suspects?" I asked Jason.

Jason shook his head. "Everyone who lives on the ranch was questioned by the sheriff and cleared."

Two little girls waved to us from their yard.

"Everyone is happy to have the Trenchcoat Twins at the ranch. You guys are famous!" Jason said. He trotted his horse past the row of houses. Ashley and I were right behind him.

I noticed a piece of yellow paper tacked to a fence. "Uh-oh," I said. "I don't think *everyone* is happy we're here."

"Why not?" Ashley asked.

I pointed to the yellow sign.

Written on it in big, black letters were the words:

TRENCHCOAT TWINS, GO HOME—OR ELSE!

Mary-Kate & Ashley
Ready for Fun and Adventure? Read All Our Books!

THE NEW ADVENTURES OF MARY-KATE & ASHLEY ™

BBO29542-X	The Case Of The Ballet Bandit	$3.99
BBO29307-9	The Case Of The 202 Clues	$3.99
BBO29305-5	The Case Of The Blue-Ribbon Horse	$3.99

THE ADVENTURES OF MARY-KATE & ASHLEY ™

BBO86369-X	The Case Of The Sea World™ Adventure	$3.99
BBO86370-3	The Case Of The Mystery Cruise	$3.99
BBO86231-6	The Case Of The Funhouse Mystery	$3.99
BBO88008-X	The Case Of The U.S. Space Camp™ Mission	$3.99
BBO88009-8	The Case Of The Christmas Caper	$3.99
BBO88010-1	The Case Of The Shark Encounter	$3.99
BBO88013-6	The Case Of The Hotel Who-Done-It	$3.99
BBO88014-4	The Case Of The Volcano Mystery	$3.99
BBO88015-2	The Case Of The U.S. Navy Adventure	$3.99
BBO88016-0	The Case Of Thorn Mansion	$3.99

YOU'RE INVITED TO MARY-KATE & ASHLEY'S ™

BBO76958-8	You're Invited to Mary-Kate & Ashley's Christmas Party	$12.95
BBO88012-8	You're Invited to Mary-Kate & Ashley's Hawaiian Beach Party	$12.95
BBO88007-1	You're Invited to Mary-Kate & Ashley's Sleepover Party	$12.95
BBO22593-6	You're Invited to Mary-Kate & Ashley's Birthday Party	$12.95

- -

Available wherever you buy books, or use this order form
SCHOLASTIC INC., P.O. Box 7502, 2931 East McCarty Street, Jefferson City, MO 65102

Please send me the books I have checked above. I am enclosing $_____ (please add
$.00 to cover shipping and handling). Send check or money order—no cash or C.O.D.s
please.

Name _____

Address_____

City_____ State/Zip_____

Please allow four to six weeks for delivery. Offer good in the U.S.A. only. Sorry, mail orders are not available to residents of Canada. Prices subject to change.

MKA1297

The Adventures of MARY-KATE & ASHLEY™

Look for the best-selling detective home video episodes.

The Case Of The Volcano Adventure™

The Case Of The U.S. Navy Mystery™

The Case Of The Hotel Who•Done•It™

The Case Of The Shark Encounter™

The Case Of The U.S. Space Camp® Mission™

The Case Of The Fun House Mystery™

The Case Of The Christmas Caper™

The Case Of The Sea World® Adventure™

The Case Of The Mystery Cruise™

The Case Of The Logical i Ranch™

The Case Of Thorn Mansion™

Join the fun!

You're Invited To Mary-Kate & Ashley's™ Camp Out Party™ *NEW*

You're Invited To Mary-Kate & Ashley's™ Ballet Party™ *NEW*

You're Invited To Mary-Kate & Ashley's™ Birthday Party™

You're Invited To Mary-Kate & Ashley's™ Christmas Party™

You're Invited To Mary-Kate & Ashley's™ Sleepover Party™

You're Invited To Mary-Kate & Ashley's™ Hawaiian Beach Party™

And also available:

Mary-Kate and Ashley Olsen: Our Music Video™

Mary-Kate and Ashley Olsen: Our First Video™

DUALSTAR VIDEO

Listen To Us!

Sleepover Party™

I am the Cute One™

Brother For Sale™

**Mary-Kate & Ashley's Cassettes and CDs
Available Now Wherever Music is Sold**

It doesn't matter if you live around the corner...
or around the world...
If you are a fan of Mary-Kate and Ashley Olsen,
you should be a member of

MARY-KATE + ASHLEY'S FUN CLUB™

Here's what you get:
Our Funzine™
An autographed color photo
Two black & white individual photos
A full size color poster
An official **Fun Club**™ membership card
A **Fun Club**™ school folder
Two special **Fun Club**™ surprises
A holiday card
Fun Club™ collectibles catalog
Plus a **Fun Club**™ box to keep everything in

To join Mary-Kate + Ashley's Fun Club™, fill out the form
below and send it along with

U.S. Residents – $17.00
Canadian Residents – $22 U.S. Funds
International Residents – $27 U.S. Funds

MARY-KATE + ASHLEY'S FUN CLUB™
859 HOLLYWOOD WAY, SUITE 275
BURBANK, CA 91505

NAME:_____

ADDRESS:_____

CITY:_____ STATE:_____ ZIP:_____

PHONE: (____) _____ BIRTHDATE:_____